To my adorable and charming nephew and niece, George and Madeline, who are much braver than I am when it comes to getting shots!

-K. P.

www.mascotbooks.com

THE LITTLE OUCH

For more information, please contact:
Mascot Books
620 Herndon Parkway, Suite 320
Herndon, VA 20170
info@mascotbooks.com

Library of Congress Control Number: 2020900369

CPSIA Code: PRT0420A
ISBN-13: 978-1-64543-436-8

Printed in the United States

The Little OUCH

KATHERINE PICARDE

ILLUSTRATED BY KHALIMA MURZINA

"I'M NOT GOING!"

I was determined.

"Penelope, we talked about this. Your doctor's appointment is in twenty minutes, and we can't be late," Dad said firmly.

Today was the day I'd been **DREADING**. I was scheduled for my annual flu shot, which is my **LEAST** favorite thing on Earth!

I tend to put on quite the performance in the doctor's office when it is time for my shot. Whenever they come near me with the Little Ouch, I start to kick my legs and flail my arms and shake my head! Then, out come the screams, louder than a siren on a police car.

"You have until the count of three to come out of your room, ready to go. One...two—"

"But Dad—the **SHOT!** It makes me **SCARED** and **NERVOUS** and **QUEASY** and **SICK** and **SWEATY** and—"

"Penelope, that's enough. We have no time for your performance today."

On the ride to the doctor's office, I thought of all the reasons why getting my flu shot was a TERRIBLE idea.

What if it hurts so bad that my arm falls off?

What if the doctor misses my arm and pokes me in the eye instead?

What if I start to feel as AWFUL as I always do?

When we got to the doctor's office, the receptionist greeted us. I could tell even SHE looked worried.

My body felt like spaghetti as I slumped down into the chair and slowly, slowly, slowly slid down toward the floor.

Then I imagined I was in a giant bubble, floating higher, higher, higher into the air. HA! No one could come near me with the Little Ouch!

"Penelope!" a nurse sang out, bursting my bubble. "I'm Nurse Lauren. You may follow me right this way."

I slithered off my chair and started my sloth-like, frightful walk toward Nurse Lauren knowing I was getting closer and closer to the Little Ouch.

She led my dad and me to an examination room where I hopped onto the table and nervously kicked my legs back and forth. Nurse Lauren started with a cheery, "Okay, Penelope! Are you ready for your—"

"NO!" I was certainly not. "You don't understand! It makes me **SCARED** and **NERVOUS** and **QUEASY** and **SICK** and **SWEATY** and—"

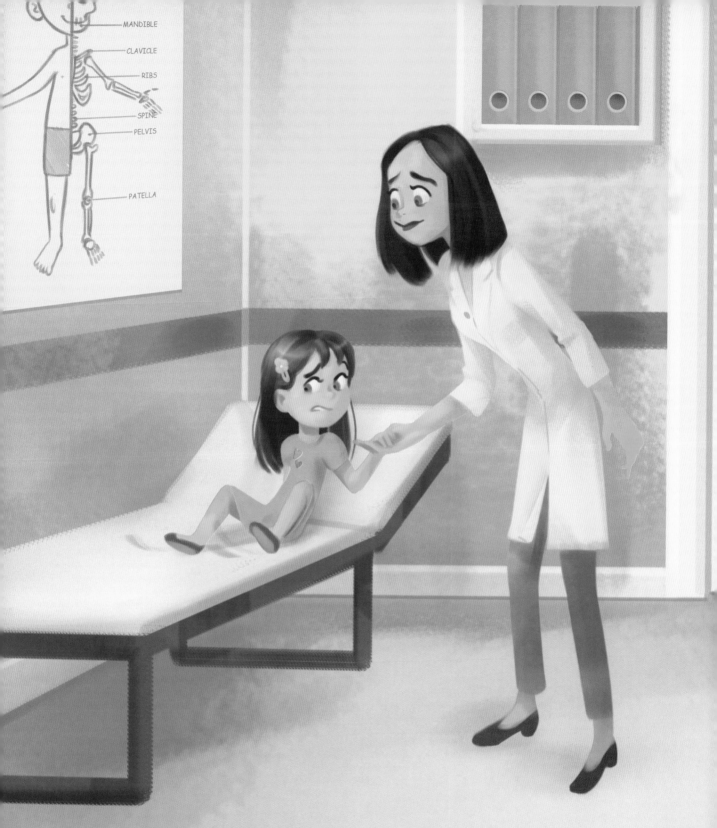

Nurse Lauren flashed a bright smile, gave my hand a gentle squeeze, and promised, "I'll be right by your side. You have nothing to fear."

"Well. . .okay. But I need to lie down." I started to lay back, but suddenly panicked. "NO! I need to sit up; no, lie down! Well, maybe sit up. Actually, lie down. Wait, sit—"

"PENELOPE!" My dad interrupted, clearly not happy with me.

"Okay," I groaned. "But, I need to go to the bathroom first."

As I wandered down the hallway, I noticed there was an empty baby stroller sitting in the waiting room. This gave me an idea...

Suddenly, two big, blue eyes and a head of crazy brown curls peered under the canopy at me and let out a very loud,

"AHHHHHH!"

Nurse Lauren and Dad found me and escorted me back to my exam room. I almost escaped the Little Ouch.

Nurse Lauren warned, "You know, Penelope, you're not going to get one of those shiny, delicious lollipops if you keep—"

"Okay, okay, okay," I finally agreed.

"Why don't you tell me a funny story?" Nurse Lauren asked.

I started talking to Nurse Lauren all about how I had mozzarella sticks for dinner last night. I told her that I was so excited to devour them, I grabbed one and shoved it in my mouth so fast that I didn't have time to realize how SCALDING hot it was!

I frantically spit it out of my mouth and onto the floor. Then, my dog sprinted by, and before I could stop him, he stuck out his tongue and scooped the mozzarella stick into his mouth in one gulp!

I was about to tell Nurse Lauren how I had to chase my dog all over the house to get that mozzarella stick out of his mouth when she announced, "Penelope, you're all set. See you next December."

"But aren't you going to give me my shot?" I asked.

"I already gave it while we were chatting about that wild mozzarella stick chase," Nurse Lauren smiled at me.

"**WHAT?!**" I couldn't believe it. Instead of getting **SCARED** and **NERVOUS** and **QUEASY** and **SICK** and **SWEATY**, I was totally **BRAVE** and **CALM** and **CHILL** and **FEARLESS** and **RELAXED!**

Nurse Lauren pressed a sparkly pink bandage over the spot where the Little Ouch had been. I hopped off the table and skipped into the waiting room. I smiled from ear to ear, knowing that I had FINALLY conquered my fear!

"Penelope!" I heard Nurse
Lauren call after me.
"Just one more thing..."

"And he stuck out his tongue and scooped the mozzarella stick into his mouth in one gulp!"

The End

About the Author

Katherine Picarde's favorite part of being a first grade teacher is seeing her students belly laugh at a good story or a funny picture book. Kat's own childhood stories and afternoons full of laughs in the classroom inspired her to write her first book, *The Little Ouch*. Her hope is that it will bring some comfort to those who are nervous for doctor's visits involving the Little Ouch. Kat remains a lifelong resident of her hometown of Medford, Massachusetts.

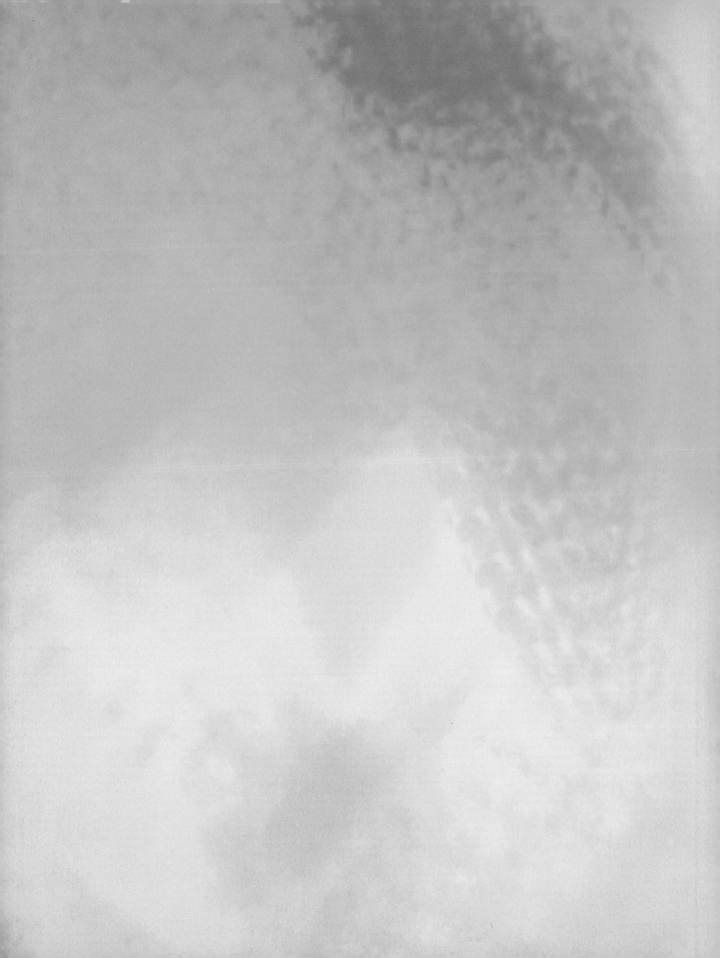

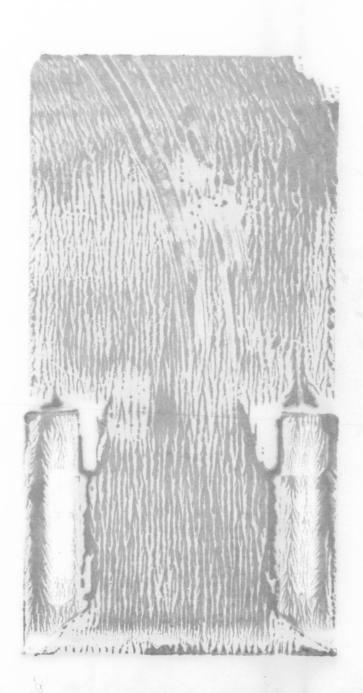

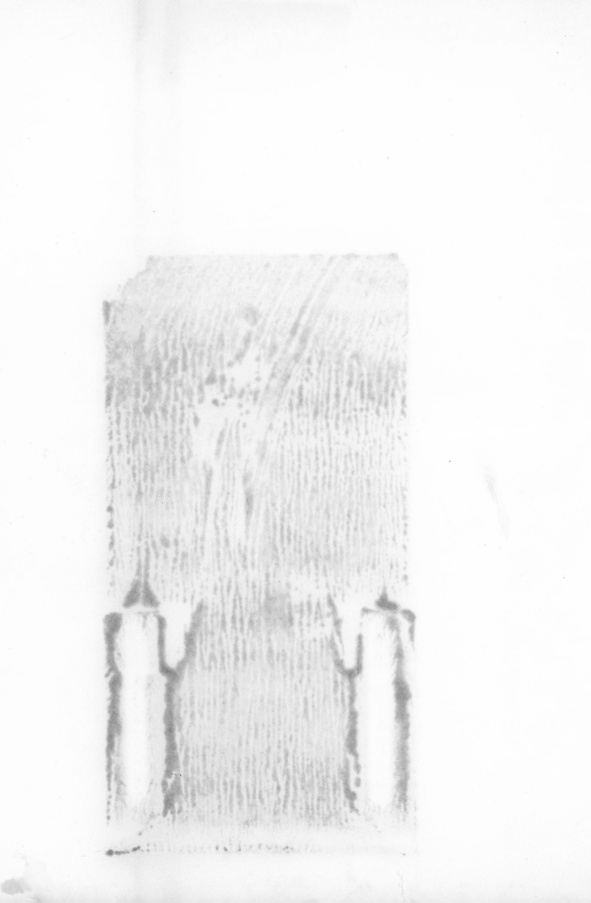

The Black Photographers Annual 1973

WITH A FOREWORD BY
TONI MORRISON
AND
AN INTRODUCTION BY
CLAYTON RILEY

Editor & Publisher	Joe Crawford
Associate Editor	Joe Walker
Picture Editors	Vance Allen, Louis Draper, Ray Francis, Beuford Smith, Shawn Walker
Designer	Vernon Grant
Editorial Assistants	Maryce Carter, Harriet Parks
Consultant	Robert L. Stewart, C.P.A.
Printing	Rapoport Printing Corp.
Binding	Sendor Bindery, Inc.
Distributor	Light Impressions, P.O. Box 3012 Rochester, N. Y. 14614

Foreword

This is a rare book: not only because it is a first, but also because it is an original idea complemented by enormous talent, energy and some of the most powerful and poignant photography I have ever seen. It was conceived as a commitment to the community of Black artists, executed as a glorious display of their craft and their perception. Consequently it is an ideal publishing venture, combining as it does necessity and beauty, pragmatism and art.

It is also a true book. It hovers over the matrix of black life, takes accurate aim and explodes our sensibilities. Telling us what we had forgotten we knew, showing us new things about ancient lives, and old truths in new phenomena.

Not only is it a true book, it is a free one. It is beholden to no elaborate Madison Avenue force. It is solely the product of its creators and its contributors. There is no higher praise for any project than that it is rare, true and free. And isn't that what art is all about? And isn't that what *we* are all about?

Toni Morrison

Introduction

In the new time, in the new space we begin to occupy, we are seeing and hearing ourselves, seeing ourselves as possessors of beauty—a re-defined sense of beauty—beginning with color, extending to shape, a new Blackness, real and strong as our history, pushing consciousness toward a new place—an understanding, a belief, the awareness of self . . . all new, perhaps, but ancient in concept.

We are confronting now the correlation between image and destiny. (Flip Wilson's comically stated premise that "what you see is what you get" is, finally, not so comic after all.)

America has prepared many lies for the general and specific population. Ours has been the myth of our ugliness. All wrong were our skin tones, ranging as they do from mahogany to cream, mis-shapen have our features been in spreading the broad nose and large lip across the map of faces descended from Africa's coastal tribes and inland royalty by way of this nation's southern ports of entry, slave markets dotting America's recent historical landscape.

Challenging these things, doing urgent battle with them, is a task, is a difficult act of special defiance, but so worthy, so deeply significant we must note and acknowledge and revere all those responsible, all those involved.

The artist, for example. The creator, the visionary, moving, doing, seeing things to be shared finally with a public too long taught to respect limitation and narrow perspectives.

The nation is surrounded by images of what it is supposed to be. And becomes institutionally and individually what those images imply, what they indicate, what they impose. The Black visual artist, his work for many years denied a true and complete public, develops muscle and emotional determination through a years-long struggle simply to be, exist and work. Thus here, in the pages beyond, an energy displayed, measures of awesome vitality and the recognition of what has always been available but hidden, an existence, a people, a whole situation and vitalized legend walking, talking, breathing in the land.

A life. Captured in tears or whatever smiles are possible whenever. A human darkness breathing an extended strength into the nation's fractured folklore. Faces, the contours of which indicate constantly the parade of events, moment to moment systems of tragic consequence, hope, loss, courage, rage, fear, the love of life and person, whatever passion may remain of the spent spirit. Lives. A freer, less distorted chronicle of our times. Other truths than the ones we have or have not been told.

In this volume then, the blood of the nation's Blood, the heart and flesh of a still-wandering tribe, traveling long and resting briefly, rarely, living the proverb: no rest for the weary.

Here, Moneta Sleet has given access to the ravished majesty of our late Lady Day, Billie Holiday who taught us to use the language, sing the song to a fuller and more expansively communicative advantage. Her arms and legs needle-pointed like a profane fabric, her eyes revealing the nearness of death, a death, ultimately, for us.

For us.

And Leisant Giraux lending to us the face of a woman as a warm Black moon in tweed jacket, ancient, patient, a globe of lost and living loves telling us in silence to keep on keepin' on.

Magnificent presences, jewels in our mythic constellation. Mahalia Jackson captured in an overpowering moment by Bert Andrews, captured as the gospel truth. Naked hand on a naked gate, a blended sexuality related by the lens and eye of Adger Cowans; two young and dreaming dancers doing an older ritual grind, and staring into a new world.—Lloyd E. Saunders

And spiritual things, too. A blur at the top of a step, as Theron Taylor bears witness to someone vanishing up some ancient (rooming-house(?)) staircase.

Our pain. Elation. Fury. The flow of human rhythms, staccato heartbeats, hands frozen into gestures of exalted and vulgar expression. Reality. Purposeful. Accidental. Amartey Dente . . . dancers. The pursuit of a language only the body translates well.

They exist here. The artists who have caught them in the process of being alive, electric, profound in their humanity.

And the masters are represented also. Roy DeCarava, priest of our culture, showing what his wise eyes have seen. James Van DerZee, as well, detailing his long encounter with these United States.

And all those who have informed the spirit here, and whom I mention, if not on these pages, then in my heart for the magnificence of their art and its impact. (In my heart where, indeed, there is more space.)

A collection, then, of the works of Black photographers, a monumental testament both to their enormous gifts, and to the people from whom they have come, the people, wondrous and strong, who have been their subjects for this study of life.

Clayton Riley

Photographers

9

Morris Rogers, Chicago, Ill.

Morris Rogers, Chicago, Ill.

Cornelius Reed, Brooklyn, N.Y.

13

Shawn Walker, Bronx, N.Y.

Hugh Grannum, Detroit, Mich.

Leisant Giraux, Brooklyn, N.Y.

Moneta Sleet, Jr., Baldwin, N.Y.

Chuck Stewart, New York, N.Y.

K. A. Morais, Bronx, N.Y.

Edward West, Albuquerque, N.M.

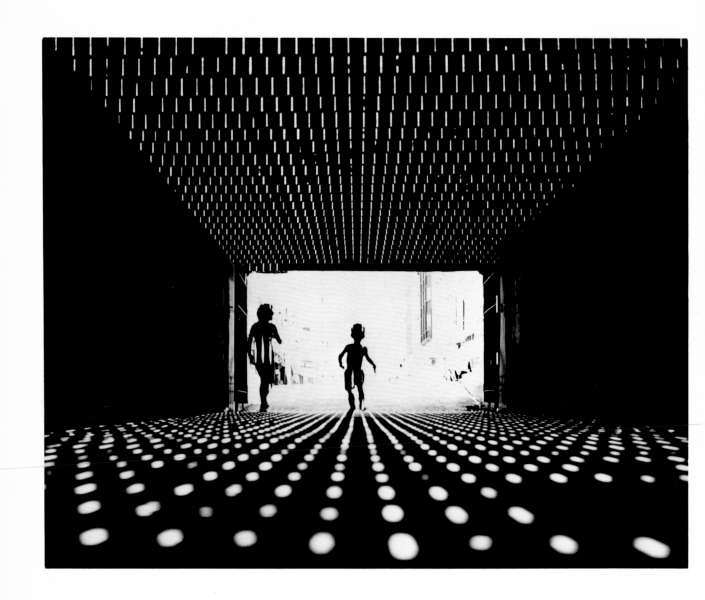

Donald R. Valentine, Hillcrest Hts., Md.

21

Leroy Henderson, Brooklyn, N.Y.

Clarence E. Eastmond, Brooklyn, N.Y.

Bert Andrews, New York, N.Y.

Lloyd E. Saunders, Chicago, Ill.

Lloyd E. Saunders, Chicago, Ill.

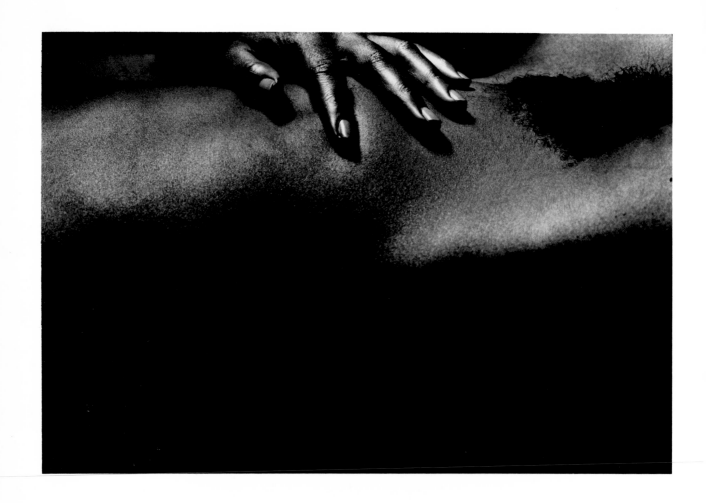

Adger Cowans, New York, N.Y.

Ray Gibson, Brooklyn, N.Y.

Theron Taylor, Denver, Colo.

29

Daniel Dawson, New York, N.Y.

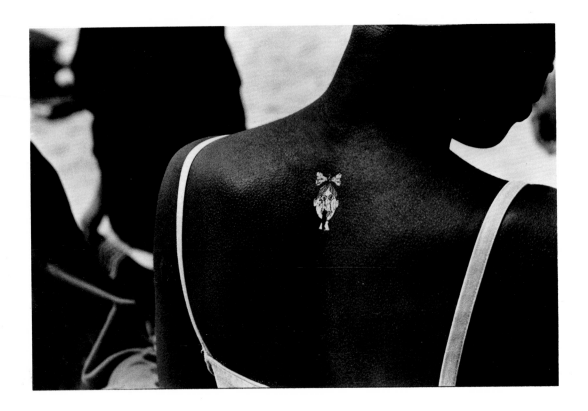

Daniel Dawson, New York, N.Y.

Daniel S. Williams, Athens, Ohio

Beuford Smith, New York, N.Y.

Roger Tucker, Newark, N.J.

Ernest Werts, Detroit, Mich.

Bill Jackson, Greenville, Miss.

Daniel Dawson, New York, N.Y.

Bob Fletcher, New York, N.Y.

Rennie George, Bronx, N.Y.

45

Ray Gibson, Brooklyn, N.Y.

Ted Williams, Hollywood, Calif.

Dorothy Gloster, New York, N.Y.

Edward West, Albuquerque, N.M.

James Mannas, Jr., Georgetown, Guyana, S.A.

Jim McDonald, Washington, D.C.

Amartey Dente, Long Island City, N.Y.

Theron Taylor, Denver, Colo.

53

Ken Beckles, New York, N.Y.

Beuford Smith, New York, N.Y.

Beuford Smith, New York, N.Y.

Rennie George, Bronx, N.Y.

Dexter Oliver, Washington, D.C.

Amartey Dente, Long Island City, N.Y.

61

Hugh Bell, New York, N.Y.

K. A. Morais, Bronx, N.Y.

Louis Draper, Bronx, N.Y.

Mel Dixon, New York, N.Y.

Portfolios

RAY FRANCIS

New Yorker Ray Francis began in photography in 1961. He has since served as a consultant to Photography for Youth Foundation and has taught photography at Pratt Institute and Bedford Stuyvesant Neighborhood Youth Corps.

In 1963 he and several other photographers founded the Kamoinge Workshop. (A New York based group of Black photographers who came together "to alleviate the atmosphere of isolation under which Black photographers operated in America of the 1960's.")

Francis is currently Director of the Multi-Media Educational T.V. Program in the Harlem school district. His photographs have been included in exhibits at Harlem's Studio Museum, Amherst College, the University of Notre Dame, the Brooklyn Museum and Harvard University. He is represented in the permanent collections of the Museum of Modern Art and the Schomburg Collection.

Ray Francis

Ray Francis

Ray Francis

MING SMITH ⋙→

New York amateur photographer Ming Smith has been
taking pictures for less than a year. She is a self-taught
photographer who was first influenced by her father.
"My photographs," she says "attempt to open the
passageway to my understanding of myself."
Her work is published here for the first time.

Ming Smith

Ming Smith

Ming Smith

Ming Smith

VANCE ALLEN

New York City photographer Vance Allen is the Editor of the James Van DerZee Institute's Photo Newsletter. He has taught photography at the Stephen Gaynor School and Brooklyn's Fort Greene Neighborhood Youth Corps.

His photographs have appeared in the New York Times, the Manhattan Tribune, the New York Courier and Liberator Magazine. "My goal in photography," he says, "is to record the human condition—the happiness, sadness, joy and beauty."

Allen's work has been exhibited, among other places, at the Metropolitan Museum of Art, Harlem's Studio Museum and Ohio University.

Vance Allen

Vance Allen

Vance Allen

ELAINE TOMLIN ⟫→

Elaine Tomlin is the National Photographer for the
Southern Christian Leadership Conference. Her
assignments have taken her to many parts of the
country to cover the civil rights struggle.

Her work, widely acclaimed and appearing in many
movement publications, has established her as one
of the movement's premier photojournalists. In
addition, her photographs have been seen in many
national publications, including Ebony, to which she
is a frequent contributor.

Elaine Tomlin

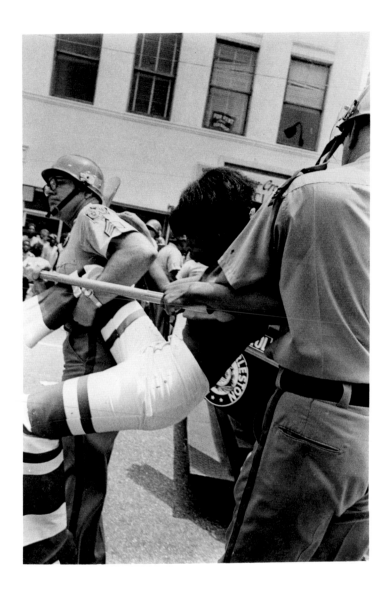

Elaine Tomlin

Elaine Tomlin

Elaine Tomlin

MONETA SLEET, JR.

Moneta Sleet has been a staff photographer for Ebony magazine for the past 17 years. On assignment he has traveled to Africa, Europe, the Soviet Union, South America, the West Indies and throughout the United States.

One of his most rewarding experiences as a photographer came in 1969 when his photograph (included in this portfolio) of Mrs. Coretta King, at the funeral service of her husband, the late Dr. Martin Luther King, Jr., won for him the Pulitzer Prize for feature photography.

He is the only Black photographer ever to win that award. Sleet, once a sportswriter for the New York Amsterdam News, switched to photography because ". . . it gave me a chance to show what it's like to be a Black man in this country."

He has had one-man exhibits at the Detroit Public Library and the City Art Museum in St. Louis, Missouri. In addition, he has been a part of many group shows.
His photographs are reproduced through the courtesy of Johnson Publications.

Moneta Sleet, Jr.

Moneta Sleet, Jr.

Moneta Sleet, Jr.

In New Bedford, Massachusetts in 1963 Tony Barboza
picked up a photo magazine and saw an ad for a
New York school of photography. He packed his bags
and headed for New York. While attending school he
worked in the studio of New York fashion photographer
Hugh Bell. In 1965 he went to the Navy where he
worked as a staff photographer. After his discharge
he went back to New York and opened his own studio.

Now a successful New York fashion photographer,
Barboza's work has appeared in many top magazines
including Harpers Bazaar, Vogue, Life, Esquire and
Essence. In addition to one-man shows at the
University of Miami, the Jacksonville Art Museum and
the Pensacola Art Museum (all in Florida), he has taken
part in many group shows.

"I want", says Barboza, "people to get a strong
feeling from my work—not necessarily the same
feeling that I get, but a strong feeling."

Anthony Barboza

Anthony Barboza

Anthony Barboza

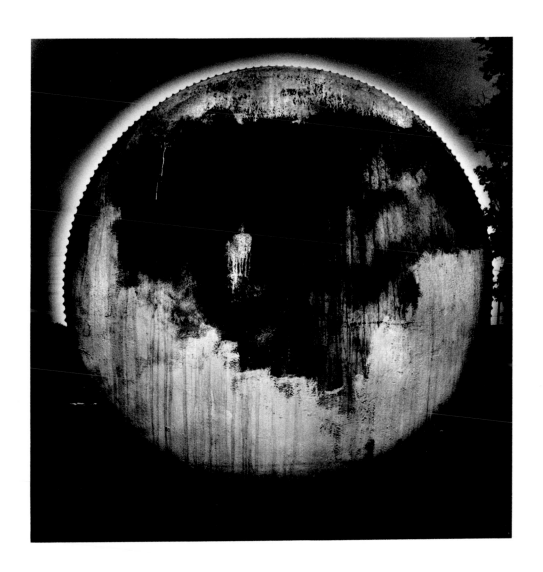

Anthony Barboza

ROY DeCARAVA

In the parlance of the photographic community master photographers are sometimes referred to as "Giants". New York photographer Roy DeCarava is a Giant.

In 1952 he was awarded a Guggenheim Fellowship for photography. He used it to ". . . satisfy my overwhelming urge to say something honest and positive about Black people." He later collaborated with the late Langston Hughes to produce the book, "The Sweet Flypaper of Life."

His one-man, 200 print exhibit at Harlem's Studio Museum was described by the Museum's Director, Edward Spriggs, as "one of the most important photo shows of our time." He has taught photography at New York's Cooper Union and is a frequent contributor to Sports Illustrated magazine.

Discussing his work in a recent interview, DeCarava states: "I just want my work to be as completely honest and as deeply emotional as I can make it." His work is in the permanent collections of the Museum of Modern Art, the Metropolitan Museum of Art, the Chicago Art Institute and many other institutions.

Roy DeCarava

Roy DeCarava

Roy DeCarava

Roy DeCarava

Roy DeCarava

Roy DeCarava

ALBERT FENNAR

New Jersey photographer Albert Fennar learned his photography in Japan and credits Japanese art and concept of design with being the most important influence on his work today.

"In the last few years", says Fennar, "I've found myself involved in the celebration of nature. My interest lies more in the visual aspects of photography than in making social comment."

Fennar has worked as a "serious amateur" for about 12 years. His work has been exhibited at the Danbury Academy of Fine Arts, the Market Place Gallery, the Fulton Art Fair, Harlem's Studio Museum and numerous other places.

Albert Fennar

Albert Fennar

Albert Fennar

When Shawn Walker returned from Cuba he
exhibited the photographs he had taken there at
Harlem's Countee Cullen Library. Of that exhibition
he said: "The reason I felt it was important to have
the exhibition was to arouse the interest of Black
people to what is happening in Cuba. I was not trying
to do a complete photo essay on Cuba, but rather
trying to show some of the impressions that I had
while there." A small sampling from that exhibit
is shown here.

Walker, a former student of Roy DeCarava, has also
exhibited at the Studio Museum, Amherst College and
Notre Dame University. His work is in the permanent
collection of the Museum of Modern Art and has been
seen in Essence, Negro World and Camera magazine.

Shawn Walker

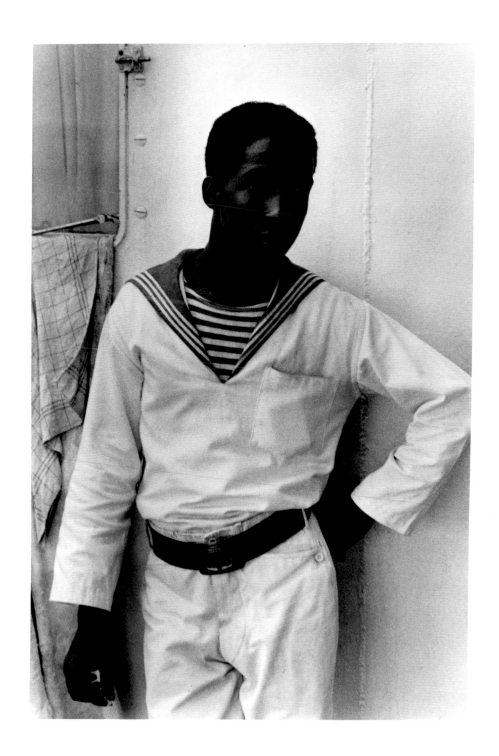

Shawn Walker

Shawn Walker

Shawn Walker

JAMES VAN DERZEE

". . . it's a hard job to get the camera to see it like you see it.
Sometimes you have it just the way you want it and then you
look in the camera and you don't have the balance. The main
thing is to get the camera to see it the way you see it."
James Van DerZee

It is amazing how many times James Van DerZee got the
camera to see it the way he did; his collection consists of
between 100 and 150 thousand prints and negatives.

Now 86, Van DerZee, an undisputed Master
Photographer, began his career at the age of 12 in Lenox,
Mass. He moved to Newark and then to New York where he
opened his first studio in Harlem. His work, spanning 6
decades, is a document of the Black experience.

His photographs of Harlem in the early 1900's made him
the main contributor to the New York Metropolitan
Museum of Art's exhibition "Harlem on My Mind." His
work has appeared in the "Black Photographer Exhibit"
and in a one-man show at the Studio Museum in Harlem.

Recently his photographs have been used extensively in
textbooks. A collection of his works, edited by Reginald
McGhee, "The World of James Van DerZee" was published
by Grove Press (1969). A new book containing his works
is scheduled for publication early in 1973.

James Van DerZee's photographs are reproduced through
the courtesy of James Van DerZee Institute, Inc.

James Van DerZee

117

James Van DerZee

James Van DerZee

James Van DerZee

James Van DerZee

121

James Van DerZee

LOUIS DRAPER

"Expressing yourself", says Louis Draper, "is really a by-product of expressing your subject. And in expressing your subject there is a coming together of those experiences that shape you and cause you to select a particular kind of material with which to work. I am concerned primarily with photography's evocative and lingering after-presence—that undefined questioning and re-examination of my environment."

Draper, a New York free lance photographer, whose work has appeared in Essence, Photography at Mid-Century, Popular Photography Annual and Camera magazine has been involved in photography for 12 years. He has studied with Harold Feinstein and W. Eugene Smith and now conducts occasional workshops himself.

His work has been exhibited at the Studio Museum, Danbury Academy of Fine Arts, George Eastman House, the Brooklyn Museum, Countee Cullen Library and numerous other places. He is represented in the permanent collection of the Schomburg Collection.

Louis Draper

Louis Draper

MIKKI FERRILL   ⟫→

Mikki Ferrill, a native Chicagoan, was born photographically 7 years ago. Previously she had attended the Art Institute of Chicago studying Advertising Design and Illustration. Upon being introduced to Ted Williams she discovered photography as a creative art form. After Ted's 13 week class of "photography combined with philosophy I began taking pictures."

Now working as a free lance photographer, she has done work for Doyle, Dane & Bernbach, J. Walter Thompson and other leading advertising agencies. In addition to a one-woman show at Chicago's Sheppard's Gallery, her work has also been seen in Life, Downbeat, Ebony, Let's Save The Children and many other publications.

"Whether it be Maxwell Street Market or a market in San Luis, Potosi, Skokie, Bronzeville, or a west side tavern," says Mikki, "I believe 'every man his own candle, and sees by his own flame'. I hope only to be able to continue to work without compromise."
"And now," she continues "as they always must, the pictures will speak for themselves."

Mikki Ferrill

Mikki Ferrill

Mikki Ferrill

Mikki Ferrill

Mikki Ferrill

"Photography is not an entity unto itself and cannot be disconnected from life. In order to give clarity to one's life and work, one must be related yet transcend the apparent, ever questioning values and ideas, relentlessly adhering to photographic responsibility, integrity and truth.

The alternative is stagnation, resulting in the popular tendency of engaging in a diarrheal discussion of filtration, miraculous developers, super fast lenses, new enlarging paper, etc. These factors are important, but represent only a means to a beginning. I believe such time consuming preoccupation stems from a reluctance to deal with the real problems of creativity and is reflective of insensitive, inhumane thinking." Herbert Randall

Herbert Randall, a former student of Harold Feinstein, works in New York as a coordinator of photography in School District No. 5. He has been the recipient of the John Hay Whitney Fellowship (1964-65) and the Creative Artists Public Service Grant (1971-72).

His work has been in many photo exhibits and is in the permanent collections of the Museum of Modern Art and the Metropolitan Museum of Art.

133

Herbert Randall

Herbert Randall

Herbert Randall

137

Herbert Randall

FRANK STEWART

Frank Stewart studied photography at Fisk University and Cooper Union. He now lives in New Rochelle, New York where he has headed the photography program of that city's Community Action Agency.

His work has been seen in the Chicago Daily Defender and in exhibits at Fisk University and the New Rochelle City Hall.

Frank Stewart

Frank Stewart

Frank Stewart

Photographer: Tom Jackson.
Mr. Jackson defines creativity
through a Minolta SR-T 101.

olta Corp. New York, N.Y.